HAPPY CHRISTMAS, HONEY!

HAPPY HONEY

HAPPY CHRISTMAS, HONEY!

written by **Laura Godwin**
pictures by **Jane Chapman**

MARGARET K. McELDERRY BOOKS
NEW YORK · LONDON · TORONTO · SYDNEY · SINGAPORE

For the children at the Caroline
School in Alberta, Canada
—L. G.

For Olivia and Georgie
—J. C.

Margaret K. McElderry Books

An imprint of Simon & Schuster Children's Publishing Division

1230 Avenue of the Americas, New York, NY 10020

Book design by Sonia Chaghatzbanian

The text of this book is set in Century Schoolbook.

The illustrations are rendered in acrylic.

Printed in the United States of America

2 4 6 8 10 9 7 5 3 1

Library of Congress Cataloging-in-Publication Data

Godwin, Laura.

Happy Christmas, Honey! / written by Laura Godwin ; pictures by Jane Chapman.

p. cm. — (Happy Honey ; 4)

Summary: Honey the cat and Happy the dog celebrate Christmas in their own way.

ISBN 0-689-84714-9

[1. Christmas—Fiction. 2. Cats—Fiction. 3. Dogs—Fiction.]

I. Chapman, Jane, ill. II. Title.

PZ7.G5438 Har 2002

[E]—dc21

2001044119

FIRST
EDITION

Christmas will come soon.
Honey wants to help.

Honey wants to help
put up the Christmas tree.

Oh, no!

No, no, Honey!

Honey wants to help
make Christmas cookies.

Oh, no!

No, no, Honey!

Honey wants to help
with the Christmas presents.

Oh, no!

No, no, Honey!

Honey wants to help
sing Christmas songs.

Fa la la la la.
Meow, meow, meow.

Oh, no!

No, no, Honey!

Come here, Honey.
Come here
and help Happy.

Happy does not want to help put up the Christmas tree.

He does not want to help make Christmas cookies.

He does not want to help
with the Christmas presents.

He does not want to help
sing Christmas songs.

Happy wants
to wait for Santa.

Will Honey help?

Honey will help Happy
wait for Santa.

But will Santa come?

Meow, meow.

Yes, Honey, yes!

Santa did come.

Woof, woof.

Happy Christmas, Honey!